THE
THREE LITTLE PIGS

with illustrations
by
Erik Blegvad

A Margaret K. McElderry Book

Atheneum   1981   *New York*

Library of Congress Cataloging in Publication Data
Three little pigs.
The three little pigs.

"A Margaret K. McElderry book."
SUMMARY: Only one of the three pig brothers
survives the hazardous experience of building a house.
[1. Folklore. 2. Pigs—Fiction] I. Blegvad,
Erik.
PZ8.1.T383 1980b   398.2′452973 [E]   80-10410
ISBN 0-689-50139-0

THE
THREE LITTLE PIGS

Once upon a time there was an old sow with three little pigs, and as she was poor and had not enough to keep them, she sent them out to seek their fortune.

The first that went off met a man with a bundle of straw and said to him, "Please, man, give me that straw to build me a house." The man did, and the little pig built a house with it.

Presently along came a wolf and knocked at the door and said, "Little pig, little pig, let me come in."

To which the pig answered, "No, no, by the hair of my chinny-chin-chin."

"Then I'll huff, and I'll puff, and I'll blow your house in," said the wolf.

So he huffed, and he puffed, and he blew the house in and ate up the little pig.

The second little pig met a man with a
bundle of sticks and said, "Please, man, give
me those sticks to build a house." The man did,
and the pig built his house.

Then along came the wolf and said, "Little pig, little pig, let me come in."

"No, no, by the hair of my chinny-chin-chin."

"Then I'll huff, and I'll puff, and I'll blow your house in."

So the wolf huffed, and he puffed, and he puffed, and he huffed, and at last he blew the house in, and he ate up the little pig.

The third little pig met a man with a load
of bricks and said, "Please, man, give me those

bricks to build a house with." The man gave him
the bricks, and he built his house with them.

The wolf came, as he had to the other little pigs, and said, "Little pig, little pig, let me come in."

"No, no, by the hair of my chinny-chin-chin."

"Then I'll huff, and I'll puff, and I'll blow your house in."

Well, he huffed, and he puffed, and he

huffed, and he puffed, and he puffed, and he

huffed; but he could *not* blow the house in.
When he found that, with all his huffing and

puffing, he could not blow the house in, he
said, "Little pig, I know where there is a nice
field of turnips."

"Where?" said the little pig.

"Oh, in Mr. Smith's field, and if you will be ready tomorrow morning, I will call for you, and we will go together and get some for dinner."

"Very well," said the little pig. "I will be ready. What time do you plan to go?"

"At six o'clock," said the wolf.

Well, the little pig got up at five and got
the turnips before the wolf came.

When the wolf came at six o'clock, he
said, "Little pig, are you ready?"

The little pig said, "Ready! I have been
there and come back again and got a nice potful
for dinner."

The wolf felt very angry at this, but he thought that he could fool the little pig somehow or other, so he said, "Little pig, I know where there is a nice apple tree."

"Where?" said the pig.

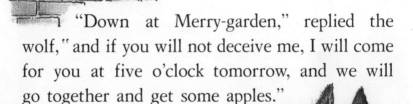

"Down at Merry-garden," replied the wolf, "and if you will not deceive me, I will come for you at five o'clock tomorrow, and we will go together and get some apples."

Well, the little pig bustled up the next morning at four o'clock and went off for the apples, hoping to get back before the wolf came.

But he had further to go, and he had to climb the tree, so that just as he was climbing down from it, he saw the wolf coming, which, as you may suppose, frightened him very much.

When the wolf came up, he said, "What, little pig! Are you here before me? Are they nice apples?"

"Yes, very," said the little pig. "I will throw you down one." And he threw it so far that, while the wolf was gone to pick it up, the little pig jumped down and ran home.

The next day the wolf came again and said to the little pig, "Little pig, there is a fair at Shanklin this afternoon. Will you go?"

"Oh, yes," said the pig, "I will go. What time shall you be ready?"

"At three," said the wolf.

So the little pig went off before the time,
as usual, and got to the fair and bought a butter
churn. He was going home with it when he saw
the wolf coming. Then he did not know what to
do. So he got into the churn to hide, and in
doing so, turned it round, and it rolled down
the hill with the pig in it. This frightened the

wolf so much that he ran home without going
to the fair.

He went to the little pig's house and told
him how frightened he had been by a great round
thing that came down the hill past him.

Then the little pig said, "Hah, I frightened you, did I! I had been to the fair and bought a butter churn, and when I saw you, I got into it and rolled down the hill."

Then the wolf was very angry indeed and declared he *would* eat up the little pig and that he would climb down the chimney after him right now.

When the little pig saw what the wolf
was about, he hung up a pot full of water and
lit a blazing fire. Just as the wolf was coming

down, he took off the cover, and in fell the
wolf. The little pig put on the cover again in
an instant, boiled him up, and ate him for
supper and lived happy ever afterwards.